WELCOME TO HOLLYWOOD!

Adapted by Ellie O'Ryan

Based on the series created by Steve Marmel

Part One is based on the episode, "Sketchy Beginnings," Written by Michael Feldman & Steve Marmel

Part Two is based on the episode, "West Coast Story," Written by Steve Marmel & Michael Feldman

DISNEP PRESS

New York

Printed in the United States of America

First Edition
1 3 5 7 9 10 8 6 4 2
J689-1817-1-09305

Library of Congress Control Number on file.
ISBN 978-1-4231-2275-3

For more Disney Press fun, visit www.disneybooks.com
Visit DisneyChannel.com

PART
ONE

CHAPTER 1

Sonny Munroe looked around in awe. She felt as if she were in a dream, so she pinched herself. *Ouch!* This definitely wasn't a dream. Sonny really was standing on the set of *So Random!*, the most popular sketch-comedy show on TV. And not only that, she was also *So Random!*'s newest cast member! Just yesterday, Sonny had been sitting at home in Wisconsin, and now here she was in Hollywood, California!

"I can't believe I'm really here!" Sonny exclaimed to her mother.

"This is so exciting!" her mom replied, just as thrilled as Sonny was. "All right, come here. Hold still." Mrs. Munroe took out a bottle of sunscreen and squirted a big glob of lotion into her palm. Then she reached for Sonny's face.

Sonny stepped back quickly. "Mom, cut it out!" she complained. "We don't need more sunblock. I'm inside!"

Her mother smiled. "I'm sorry," she said. "It's not every day I hand my beautiful daughter over to show business."

"Look, Mom, we talked about all this," Sonny said patiently. "Show business is *not* going to change me. I'm the same girl here that I was back in Wisconsin."

"There she is!" a voice suddenly boomed. "There's my new star!"

Sonny and her mom turned around and

found themselves face-to-face with Marshall Pike, the executive producer of *So Random!* Marshall was a short, balding man who wore a cell-phone headset wherever he went. He was *very* important—and Sonny could hardly believe that he was talking to her!

"Mr. Pike!" she exclaimed.

"Please, it's Marshall," he replied smoothly. "Connie, wonderful to see you again, too," he said, giving Sonny's mother a nod. "We're so thrilled to have Sonny join our family. Oh, and I promise you, she's in very good hands here."

"Good," Mrs. Munroe said. "Because you know what we do in Wisconsin to people who make promises they can't keep?"

"You make them into cheese?" joked Marshall. "I can see where Sonny gets her sense of humor," he added pleasantly.

Sonny spoke up. "Actually, I get it from my dad. She's not kidding." Then she looked directly at her mom. "But she *is* hovering."

"All right, I can take a hint," Mrs. Munroe said. "Someone wants their mom to leave. Come here before I go." She reached out to give her daughter a hug. "I know I've said this a million times, but—"

"Don't talk to strangers?" Sonny finished her mother's sentence.

"No," Mrs. Munroe replied. "But, yes."

"Don't swim after eating?" Sonny asked.

"I'm trying to tell you how proud I am of you!" Mrs. Munroe exclaimed. She tenderly patted Sonny's cheeks. "I just couldn't be prouder."

"You just put a little more sunblock on me, didn't you?" Sonny asked suspiciously.

"No," her mom said. "But, yes," she admitted.

Sonny rolled her eyes, but she gave her mother a big hug. Then she watched as her mom walked away. She could be a little overprotective sometimes, but Sonny wouldn't know what to do without her.

Sonny took a deep breath and smiled. On the other side of the *So Random!*–set doors was a new life for her. And she couldn't wait for it to begin!

CHAPTER 2

After Mrs. Munroe left, Marshall gave Sonny a tour of the studio. "Here we are, kiddo," he said as he held a door open for Sonny. "This is the prop house."

Sonny couldn't believe her eyes as she stepped into a room that was packed with all the props she'd seen in her favorite *So Random!* TV sketches. And now she was getting to see them in person!

"Oh, my gosh!" she exclaimed as she looked

around. "This is so cool! I've read about this place—this is where the cast hangs out." She ran over to another corner of the room. "This is the gnome from the 'Gnome' sketch! And that's the sarcophagus from the 'Mummy Dearest' sketch! And that's a pink hat . . ." Sonny paused. "That I've never seen before."

"Yep, one day there will be props in here from sketches you were in. Maybe one of your hats," Marshall said. "Anyway, just know, as executive producer, I'm always here for you."

"Marshall, your mother is on line four," Marshall's assistant announced over the speaker system.

"Take a message," Marshall replied.

"*And* five," added the assistant.

Marshall's eyes widened—his mother on *two* lines?! "I've got to go," he told Sonny as he rushed out of the room.

That left Sonny alone in the prop house. A

grin spread across her face as she started to explore it, checking out all the cool props. Each one had its own special history on *So Random!* She decided to start with the sarcophagus, the spooky, human-size Egyptian coffin. Slowly, Sonny opened its decorated cover—and found someone inside!

"Ahhhh!" Sonny shrieked.

"Ahhhh!" the girl inside the coffin yelled back. "Don't you knock?" she asked when she had caught her breath. Sonny had never met the girl before, but she knew exactly who she was: Zora Lancaster, the youngest, but also one of the funniest cast members of *So Random!*

"Sorry!" Sonny cried. "I didn't realize anyone was here. But you're Zora, and I'm Sonny. I'm new."

"Obviously, otherwise you would have knocked," Zora replied with a huff. "Now, if you don't mind—" she said, and swung the coffin closed.

Sonny smiled. Zora was just as wacky as she'd hoped!

Just then, two people in the middle of an intense debate walked into the prop house. They were Grady Mitchell and Nico Harris, two other cast members.

Sonny looked at them curiously. Grady was wearing the bottom half of an egg costume, and Nico was dressed like a chicken. Sonny couldn't wait to figure out what *this* was about.

"How come *you* get to be the chicken?" Grady complained as he tried to squeeze through the doorway. His giant egg costume was making it rather difficult.

"Because *I* have more of a chicken body and *you* have more of an egg body," explained Nico.

"Hey, guys!" Sonny interrupted as she stepped forward. She held out her hand for them to shake.

11

Both boys turned to look at her.

"Hello, there," Nico said suavely as he kissed Sonny's outstretched hand. "I'm Nico. But you knew that."

"Grady," Grady butted in. "But you knew that."

"And I'm Sonny. But I knew that," Sonny joked.

"Wait a minute," Grady said. "You're that funny girl from the Internet!" Sonny smiled, flattered that Grady knew who she was and that he'd seen the videos of her comedy sketches that she'd posted online.

Just then, a pretty blond girl walked into the room. She was carrying a magazine. "Hey, everyone," she said breezily. "Did you see? I'm on the cover of *Tween Weekly*. Again!"

"We're *all* on the cover," Nico pointed out.

"Really? Because all I see is me," the girl retorted.

Sonny couldn't contain her excitement any longer. Here, at last, was her chance to meet Tawni Hart—the longest-running cast member of *So Random!*

"Hi, Tawni!" she exclaimed. "I just wanted to say I am *such* a huge fan! Honestly, you've been a role model for me and my friends back in Wisconsin! We kind of feel like you're one of us. I'm Sonny!" Sonny stopped speaking and threw her arms around Tawni, giving her a big hug.

"Why am I being touched?" Tawni asked coldly, her arms rigid at her side.

"Sorry," Sonny said, smiling sheepishly. "I'm a hugger."

"Small world," Nico said, extending his arms. "So am I!"

Before Sonny—or Tawni—could respond, Marshall walked back into the prop house. "I see you've met everyone," he said, smiling at Sonny.

"Yes, and I just want to say, it is such an honor for me to be here, working with you guys," Sonny said, beaming at the cast.

Ignoring Sonny, Tawni turned to Marshall. "Marshall, what does she mean, *'working with'* us?" she asked suspiciously.

"Well, she's our newest cast member, Tawni," he told her. "Remember? We said good-bye to Mandy on our last show?"

"I remember the good-bye," Tawni replied. "I just didn't think there was going to be a *hello*."

"He showed us her Web site," Nico reminded Tawni.

"And we all got her photo," added Zora. "Remember?"

Tawni remembered the photo, all right. She remembered drawing a giant mustache on Sonny's face and throwing darts at it.

Tawni widened her eyes innocently. "Nope. Don't remember. But welcome aboard!"

14

"That's the attitude, Tawni," Marshall said with relief. "You two are going to be fast friends. Hey, as a matter of fact, you can give Sonny the tour!"

Sonny gasped excitedly. "I would love that!" she responded. She couldn't wait to bond with her new castmate.

Tawni rolled her eyes. That was the last thing she wanted to do. "Let's go, *Someone*-y," she said as she stalked across the room.

"It's Sonny," Sonny called as she hurried to keep up with Tawni. She smiled to herself. "My first day in Hollywood and I've already got a nickname!" she said happily.

Tawni begrudgingly led Sonny through the studio. "Okay, the tour is starting. Keep up. This is where I get my snacks," she said in a bored tone. "This is where I learn. And this is a camera, which *loves* me."

Then Tawni led Sonny into a large room that

was divided in half. On one side was Tawni's dressing area, filled with different costumes, accessories, and all sorts of makeup. On the other side was a workout area packed with gym equipment.

"And finally, this is where I do my costume changes, my makeup, my preshow chillaxing . . ." Tawni said as she walked behind a curtain.

"Cool!" Sonny replied. "So where do *I* do my preshow chillaxing?"

"I'm sorry, this concludes our tour," Tawni replied haughtily as she walked out from behind the curtain wearing a pink velour tracksuit and a pair of sneakers.

"Wow, you're a fast changer," Sonny said.

"And you're a slow leaver," Tawni quipped, rolling her eyes.

"You think *I'm* a slow leaver, you should have seen my mom this morning. I couldn't get her to leave!" Sonny said with a laugh.

Tawni gave Sonny a blank stare and then turned around, ignoring her.

Sonny continued. "So, you wouldn't happen to know where my dressing room is, would you?" she asked Tawni, who had started doing warm-up exercises. Tawni stretched her arms and kicked her legs—suspiciously close to Sonny's face.

"Wow! I don't want to interrupt your work-out, or anything. You've got quite a wingspan there!" Sonny exclaimed as she ducked to avoid being kicked. "You know, if I didn't know any better, I'd think you were trying to kick me in the face." She chuckled good-naturedly.

Suddenly, Zora popped her head out of a vent near the ceiling. "Zora smells trouble!" she called out.

"What's up there?" Sonny asked as she looked up curiously at her castmate.

"Right now, the best seat in the house," Zora said, laughing. She grabbed a handful of popcorn. "As you were," she said, motioning for Tawni and Sonny to carry on.

Tawni picked up a small barbell. "For some reason, she prefers to live up there like a common bat, rather than down here with *me*," she informed Sonny.

"Yeah, that's a real brainteaser," cracked Zora.

Just then, there was a knock at the door. It was Marshall. "I just wanted to see how you're settling in," he said to Sonny.

But as he looked around, a frown suddenly crossed Marshall's face. "Why is there gym equipment on Sonny's side of the room?" he asked Tawni suspiciously.

"This is *my* side of the room?" Sonny asked, surprised.

"This is *her* side of the room?" Tawni said.

"Don't you remember?" Marshall replied, trying to remain patient. "I was very clear when Mandy left that Sonny would get this side of the room."

Tawni remembered, all right. She also remembered lugging the gym equipment to Sonny's side of the room.

She gave Marshall an innocent look. "Nope, doesn't ring a bell," she lied.

"All right. Well, we'll get all this equipment back to the studio gym, and give Sonny some space," Marshall said as he started to leave the room. He paused at the door. "I can feel the chemistry already!" he told the girls. He smiled at them and walked away.

Sonny took one look at the angry expression on Tawni's face and quickly said, "It's okay! I can make this work. I'm a make-do kind of person. Watch me make do! I'll just put my jacket right here." She hung her jacket on the handles of the treadmill, and then rested her guitar against another piece of equipment. "And I'll just chillax right here!" Sonny said brightly as she leaned against the elliptical trainer.

19

But nothing she said—or did—softened the angry look on Tawni's face. Sonny was at a loss for what to do next.

"My making-do isn't really working, is it?" she asked.

"No," Tawni replied flatly.

"Want to talk about it?" Sonny asked hopefully.

"Sure," Tawni told her sweetly. "Grab a seat," she said, giving Sonny a fake smile.

Sonny searched for a place to sit, but she couldn't find one that wasn't covered with Tawni's costumes, Tawni's makeup, or Tawni's accessories. So Sonny plunked down on the floor as Tawni grabbed her favorite stuffed animal, a fluffy white cat.

"Comfortable, roomie?" asked Tawni in a syrupy-sweet voice.

Sonny tried to relax. "Less so by the minute," she said nervously.

"Let's think of this studio as a school," continued Tawni. She stared at Sonny coldly. "I'm the head cheerleader, and you're the new kid. And you're all gung-ho and wanting to join the squad. You've got all these great ideas, and you're full of enthusiasm—"

"Yeah!" interrupted Sonny. "That's right! I am!"

"Well, knock it off," Tawni snapped. "You're not wanted on the squad."

"But I'm already on the squad," Sonny pointed out.

"Yes, but we don't *need* you on the squad," Tawni replied. Then she turned back to her stuffed animal. "Do we, Puddy Two-Shoes?" she asked the cat.

"*Puddy Two-Shoes*?" Sonny asked incredulously. She couldn't believe that was actually the name of Tawni's stuffed cat!

Tawni ignored her. "And we *certainly* don't

want to hear your cheers. Not your 'sis' or your 'boom' or your 'bah.'" She gave Sonny a pointed look.

"But what if I have a really awesome 'bah'?" asked Sonny, trying to lighten the mood.

"I don't care if it's the greatest 'bah' since . . . Sheep Independence Day," Tawni said with a scowl. "So stay on your side, don't touch my stuff, and keep out of my spotlight!" she cried angrily. Then, with a total attitude change, she said brightly, "Okay, then. Let's go rehearse."

Sonny watched in silence as Tawni dropped her stuffed cat and stalked out of the room. Then Sonny turned to Puddy Two-Shoes. "If you could talk, would you scream?" she asked, letting out a deep sigh.

She was starting to feel more than just a little frustrated by Tawni and her divalike behavior. How could her first day on the set be turning into such a disaster? Sonny sighed. She knew she needed to look on the bright side. The day will probably get better, she thought. After all, it couldn't possibly get any worse!

CHAPTER
3

Later that day, Sonny found herself in the middle of a swarm of activity. Several stagehands were transforming a soundstage into a beehive set, complete with honeycomb walls and sticky honeypots. Just then, Nico and Grady bumbled onto the stage wearing yellow and black worker-bee costumes.

"You happy now?" Nico asked Grady. "Exact same costumes."

"How come your wings are bigger?" Grady

asked, eyeing his castmate's costume.

"Your antennae are longer," Nico quickly pointed out.

"The good thing is, you both have the same size brains," Marshall commented, overhearing their conversation. He shook his head. So much drama all the time! "Okay, people, let's start rehearsing Tawni's 'Queen Bee' sketch," he said, calling the cast to order.

Just then, Zora flitted over to Sonny. Both girls were also wearing worker-bee costumes. "I heard you got the whole 'sis, boom, bah' speech," Zora whispered.

"People are talking about that already?" Sonny whispered back. She hated to be the focus of gossip on her very first day!

"No, no—I was eavesdropping," replied Zora. "It's kind of my thing right now. That and revenge. Want to get some?"

Sonny shook her head. "No. This is Tawni's

25

sketch. She's the queen bee—I'm just a worker bee. I'm going to lay low, stay out of her way, and mind my own *buzz*-ness." She giggled at her own joke.

"All right. Places, everybody!" Marshall called out.

Everybody scrambled to their place on set and the rehearsal began. Tawni sat on a large throne, tossing her head so that her jeweled crown sparkled in the bright lights.

"The good knights approach!" Zora announced, and trumpet fanfare followed.

"Hello, good knights!" Tawni said as Nico and Grady walked into the scene.

"Good *night*? But it's two in the afternoon," Nico said, pretending to be confused.

"No, not good *night*," Grady corrected him. "Good *knight*."

"Silence!" Tawni commanded.

Marshall buried his head in his hands.

"Which is exactly what we're going to hear if the audience watches this sketch. Stop! Cut! This isn't working!" he shouted.

"I agree," Tawni said. "What is everybody else doing wrong?"

"Kids," Marshall said, shaking his head, "this sketch stinks. What are we going to do?" He looked around, hoping that someone had a good suggestion.

Sonny raised her hand to speak up. But before she could say anything, Tawni shot her a dirty look.

"Maybe the *problem* is that there's one too many bees," Tawni snapped, staring directly at Sonny.

Sonny meekly lowered her hand.

"No, that's not it. We've got to think bigger . . . bolder . . . some other *b* word," Marshall replied.

"I got it!" Nico suddenly yelled out. His castmates looked at him hopefully. "What we need is a swimming pool filled with honey!"

Zora shook her head. "Whenever you say you 'got it,' you *never* got it," she told Nico.

"How about you, new girl?" Marshall said to Sonny. He had noticed that she had raised her hand earlier. "You got something?"

"Um . . . I *might* got something," Sonny said timidly.

"Go on," Marshall said encouragingly.

"Yes. Please, sprinkle us with your Wisconsin funny dust," Tawni added sarcastically.

"Well . . ." Sonny said cautiously. "What if Tawni was, like, a clumsy bee . . . you know, like a bumbling bee?"

Nico and Grady chuckled, and Tawni glared at them.

"And then we could get distracted by things that bees get distracted by, like . . . flowers," Sonny continued, pointing at some props. "Because, you know, we love flowers!" She ran over to a large bouquet and buried her face in it, sending petals and stems everywhere.

"That's terrible." Tawni snorted.

"Terribly *good*," Marshall corrected her. "What else have you got?" he asked, turning back to Sonny.

"Well, what else do bees love?" Sonny asked, encouraged by Marshall's enthusiasm.

"They love to sting things!" Zora piped up excitedly.

"Yes!" Sonny exclaimed. "Okay, well, what if an old lady walks in with a really huge butt?" Sonny launched into an impression of someone with a gigantic rear end.

"That's great!" Grady cried. "Because old-lady butts make great targets."

"Okay, so she walks over . . . *Boom! Boom! Boom!*" Sonny continued as she waddled over to the flowers. "Then she sees a penny. . . ." Sonny bent over, sticking her bottom in the air.

Then she put on her best old-lady voice. "The all-you-can-sting *butt*-fet is open!" she announced.

Everyone laughed hysterically—well, everyone except Tawni. She was not pleased that the new girl was getting so much attention.

"That's beautiful! I love it!" Marshall cheered. "Queen bee's out; bumbling bee's in. Lunch!" he shouted, heading off the set.

Most of the cast and crew scurried offstage, following behind Marshall. That left just Tawni and Sonny. As Tawni stared at her with a look of pure hatred, Sonny gulped. If looks could kill, Sonny knew exactly what she'd be: a dead bumblebee.

"Do you want to *buzz* over and get some lunch?" Sonny asked nervously.

But Tawni just turned and stormed away.

Sonny was left alone, feeling more worried than ever. She had come up with a great new skit, but she had also dethroned the queen bee. Now she had to figure out a way to make sure the sketch went well *and* repair things with Tawni. She certainly had her work cut out for her!

CHAPTER 4

That night, Sonny curled up in a big armchair in the living room. She and her mom had just moved into their new apartment, and it still didn't feel quite like home. To make matters worse, Sonny couldn't stop thinking about how she was going to fix things with Tawni. She hadn't come up with anything!

"Honey, look at this!" Sonny's mom said excitedly as she pulled items out of a bag. "Oranges, avocados, *and* tube socks—all purchased from a guy standing on a freeway off-ramp. I didn't even have to get out of the car. What a town!"

"Well, at least one of us had a good day," Sonny said glumly.

"Oh, come on—was it that bad?" her mom asked.

"Let me put it this way—you slapping sunscreen on my face was the highlight," Sonny replied. "Marshall is making me do this bee sketch with Tawni, and she *hates* me."

"Do you want me to write a note?" asked her mother.

Sonny shook her head. As if a note from her mother was going to help this situation!

Mrs. Munroe put an arm around her daughter. "Honey, when you're chasing your dreams, there are always going to be bumps in the road. We didn't travel all the way from Wisconsin for you to give up on your very first day."

"I didn't say I was giving up," Sonny replied.

"That's the spirit!" her mom cheered. "Look, I'll tell you what to do. Go down there tomorrow and you talk to Tawni," she advised her daughter.

Sonny sighed. Maybe her mother was right. Well, I guess I'll just have to wait and see, she thought.

The next morning, Sonny walked into the dressing room ready to apologize to Tawni.

"Get away from me," Tawni snapped as she fed sheets of paper into a shredder.

"Tawni, come on," pleaded Sonny. "I'm trying to apologize. I really feel bad about getting off on the wrong foot, and I was thinking maybe we could start fresh—" Sonny stopped when she saw what Tawni was doing. "Are you shredding fan mail?" she asked, confused.

"Not *mine*," Tawni said with a smirk. "Done with Grady's. Where's the Nico pile?" Tawni looked around, then noticed a wrapped present. "What's this?"

"I got you a little something to say, 'I'm sorry,'" Sonny replied, nudging the present toward her castmate.

Tawni ripped open the box. Inside was a stuffed cat.

"It's a fuzzy little friend for Puddy Two-Shoes!" Sonny said cheerfully. "You know, a peace offering."

"Aw," Tawni said sweetly. "A peace offering." She grabbed the stuffed animal and jammed it into the paper shredder. Bits of white fur and stuffing flew into the air. "Now it's a *million-piece* offering."

Sonny's mouth dropped open. She was starting to lose her patience. She took a deep breath. "Look, you don't have to forgive me, but we still have to do that bee sketch together," she told her.

35

"Not going to happen," Tawni replied, fixing her makeup in the mirror.

Then Sonny had an idea. There was one way to get through to Tawni that she hadn't tried yet. "But I just want to be as good in my first show as you are in every show," she said. "You have so much to teach me, and I have so much to learn."

"Flattery won't get you *anywhere*," Tawni said with a toss of her head.

"You're the funniest and prettiest one on the show," Sonny said, trying again.

Suddenly, Tawni turned around to face Sonny. "My approach to comedy is simple . . ." she began, with a total change in attitude.

Sonny smiled. It looked like her plan was going to work!

That afternoon, Sonny and Tawni sat together on the set. Tawni was still rambling on about acting.

"If we're going to be those bumbling bees of yours, here's something you need to know about me—I don't play bumbling bees."

"That's okay! Because I've got a million ideas," Sonny replied. "I'm just glad we're finally getting along better."

Just then, Nico and Grady walked on to the set. "Oh, so you're working on Sonny's sketch?" Nico asked the girls. Sonny winced. That was the worst thing he could have said.

"No, no," she quickly corrected him. "It's *our* sketch."

But the damage was already done. Tawni's face twisted into an ugly scowl. "It used to be *my* sketch. Used to be *my* dressing room. Used to be *my* show!" she cried.

Nico and Grady started to back away. They didn't want to get involved—especially not when Tawni had *that* look on her face and *that* tone of voice.

"No," Sonny said nervously. "Remember? We're *bees*! We're happy, happy bees!"

"Fine. We're bees," Tawni snipped as she grabbed Sonny's bee costume off the table. "Let's say a new bee arrived at the hive. And on her first day she *buzzed* in, and she thought she knew everything, threw out one of her millions of ideas, and stung the queen right in the back!" she shouted. "How would that make you feel?"

Tawni stabbed the stinger of Sonny's bee costume into the table to illustrate her point. But she missed—and stabbed her own hand instead!

"*Ow!*" Tawni shrieked. She ran off to her dressing room, with Sonny following right behind her.

"I can't believe you stabbed me!" Tawni cried dramatically.

"I didn't stab you!" protested Sonny. "You stabbed yourself!"

38

"You just stood there and watched, which is just like stabbing, so it's really *your* fault. I *knew* you were out to get me!" Tawni said accusingly.

Sonny sighed. "I'm not out to get you," she said patiently. "Here, we need to rinse that out." She placed Tawni's hand under the faucet and turned the knob.

Whoosh!

Suddenly, a gush of scalding water poured out of the tap!

"*Ahhhhhh!*" Tawni screamed.

"Oh, my gosh!" Sonny cried. "Sorry! We need ointment—and a bandage!" Sonny looked around frantically but didn't see any gauze, so she grabbed the first piece of fabric she saw and started tearing it into thin strips. But what she didn't realize was that the fabric she was ripping was actually the cape from Tawni's queen-bee costume.

"That's my favorite cape!" Tawni howled. "How *could* you?"

Sonny was getting desperate to make things better. She hoped a little humor might help the situation. "How many capes do you have?" she joked. She started to wrap strips of the cape around Tawni's hand as a bandage. "Here we go," she said, trying to get Tawni to stay still.

"You're out of your mind!" Tawni yelled, jumping up. "Get away from me!"

But Sonny wanted to make things right—somehow. "Sorry. Here, take Puddy," she suggested, holding out the stuffed cat to Tawni. "Puddy makes everything better!"

"Don't touch my Puddy!" ordered Tawni. She grabbed Puddy out of Sonny's hands so forcefully that the stuffed animal flew through the air—right toward the paper shredder!

Sonny could barely watch. It was as if everything happened in slow motion, from

Tawni's drawn-out scream of *"Puuuuuuuuuu-ddddddddddyyyyyyyy!"* to the grinding of the machine as it shredded her beloved stuffed animal into a million pieces.

Sonny cringed. One thing was for sure: the situation with Tawni had just gotten worse—about a *million* times worse!

CHAPTER 5

Moments later, Sonny found herself sitting in Marshall's office with a fuming Tawni. Sonny's first episode of *So Random!* was just hours away; the bee sketch still needed work; and Tawni was being more difficult than ever. The situation couldn't really be any worse.

"*Look* at me," Tawni moaned. "I'm covered in Puddy!"

"I'm sorry," Sonny said miserably. She couldn't believe what had just happened. This is definitely not going to win me any brownie points with Tawni, she thought.

"'Sorry' isn't going to bring Puddy back, is it?" asked Tawni angrily. She knew Sonny should have never joined the cast!

"We'll get you a new Puddy Two-Shoes," Marshall said soothingly. "A better Puddy Two-Shoes. We'll get you a Puddy *Three-Shoes*!"

"Well, what about my pride?" Tawni asked. "That's been shredded, too."

"Look, Tawni, the last thing I ever wanted to do was hurt your pride," Sonny replied. "And if I did, I'm really sorry. But now I just want to make things better." She turned to Marshall. "Marshall, do you think you can add the queen-bee sketch back in the show?" she asked eagerly. Maybe this would be the way to fix things!

Marshall shook his head. "I think the

43

bumbling-bee sketch is funnier," he admitted, shrugging his shoulders.

"I don't," Tawni retorted. "And let's see how funny it is *without* me."

"But I can't do the sketch without you!" Sonny cried.

"Then I guess, just like Puddy, the sketch is no longer with us," Tawni said with a sniff. She dabbed at her tears with a tissue.

Sonny stared at Tawni. "You know that Puddy was a stuffed—"

But Tawni wouldn't let her finish. *"La la la la la!"* she sang, clapping her hands over her ears dramatically. Clearly, Puddy *wasn't* just a stuffed animal to her.

"Okay, that's it," Sonny said, finally losing her patience. "Ever since I got here, I've been walking on eggshells trying to keep the head cheerleader happy, but apparently that's impossible!" she exclaimed, her voice getting louder and louder.

"And you know what? I can 'sis,' and I can 'boom,' and my 'bah' kicks butt, thank you very much! Because I am one bad bee!" she finished.

But then Sonny stopped yelling. A thought had just occured to her. "Oh, my gosh! 'One Bad Bee!' I've got an idea for the sketch and it *doesn't* involve Tawni. I have to go. *Sis, boom, bye!*" she shouted, running out of the room.

"You go, girl!" Marshall called after Sonny as she ran out of the room. Then he turned to Tawni with a frown on his face. "You can go, too," he told her.

Just a few hours later, Sonny was ready to make her debut on *So Random!* The cameras were rolling, the set was ready, and out in the darkness sat a real live audience, waiting for the sketch to begin.

Here we go, Sonny thought, taking a deep breath.

Suddenly, the beehive set was flooded with light. The announcer's voice rang through the studio. "Let's get back to *So Random!*," he exclaimed.

Zora, Nico, and Grady shimmied onto the set, dressed as cheerleader bees. They started to dance hip-hop style as they chanted, *"Sis, boom, buzz! Sis, boom, buzz! Sis, boom, buzzity-buzz!"*

Sonny stepped onto the set, and a spotlight shone directly on her. She was ready to wow the audience!

As the other cast members continued their background beat, Sonny started to rap:

> *I'm just the new bee, and it's hard to fit in,*
> *When the queen bee has the thinnest skin!*
> *No matter how nice you try to be,*
> *She's always "Me me me me me!"*

Sonny did a quick dance move, ending with a step backward. But she accidentally backed into Nico—and stung him with her stinger! Oops, Sonny thought. Totally didn't mean to do that!

"Ow!" he yelped.

"Sorry!" Sonny whispered. Then she continued with her solo. After all, the cameras were still rolling.

> I try to be nice,
> But see what it gets?
> It's like jamming a stick inside a
>   hornet's nest.
> I'm not a stumbling bee, a crumbling bee.
> A tumbling, a fumbling, or mumbling bee.
> A jumbling bee!
> A rumbling bee!
> I guess the only bee that I can be is—me!

Sonny struck a pose as she finished her song. She grinned out at the audience—who burst into applause! Sonny breathed a sigh of relief. She had nailed her first performance! I'll never forget this moment! she thought.

As the lights dimmed, Sonny, Nico, Grady, and Zora scurried offstage for one last costume change. Then they returned to the set for the big sign-off. The show was almost over. Scowling, Tawni joined them.

Marshall hurried onto the set. "Okay, people! Great show!" he whispered happily. "Coming back to the sign-off in five." He turned to Sonny. "Nice job out there tonight, kiddo. And since it's your first show, why don't you say the good night?" he suggested.

"*What?*" Sonny asked in shock. She couldn't believe that Marshall was going to honor her with the sign-off!

"What?" echoed Tawni. She also couldn't

48

believe that Sonny was going to get to do the sign-off.

But there was no time for Sonny to panic—or for Tawni to protest. Marshall ran off the stage, calling, "In four, three . . ."

Light filled the set once more. The whole cast smiled at the camera. Sonny took a deep breath and continued to smile, trying to contain her nervousness.

"Well, that's our show, everybody," Sonny began. "And I just want to say that for as long as I can remember, this has been a dream of mine. Meeting the boys, hanging with Zora . . ." Sonny paused. Out of the corner of her eye, she could see how hard Tawni was trying to hide her disappointment.

"And best of all," Sonny continued, "getting to work with one of my true heroes, and the inspiration for that last sketch—give it up for Tawni Hart!" As she spoke, Sonny flung her arm out to gesture toward Tawni.

Smack!

Sonny's outstretched hand clocked Tawni square in the face, and Tawni fell to the ground!

Sonny looked down at Tawni in horror. That was *not* the way she wanted to end her first episode of *So Random!* But she knew that the show must go on.

"Well, that's our show, everybody," she said quickly. "Good night!"

CHAPTER 6

The cameras had stopped rolling. The audience had already left. But Sonny and the cast of *So Random!* were still totally pumped. Well, most of the cast. As soon as the show had ended, Tawni stalked to her dressing room and refused to come out. And Zora, well, no one was really sure where she ran off to. But the excitement of performing hadn't worn off for Sonny, Grady, and Nico, as they laughed and joked in the prop house, celebrating a great show. Sonny couldn't believe how well it had turned out. She could not stop smiling.

Grady's voice rose above the chatter. He turned to Sonny. "So, we have a tradition on *So Random!*: the first time you star in a sketch, you get to hang up a prop in the prop house," he explained.

Sonny looked at him curiously and then thought for a moment. Then she held up the bee antennae she'd worn in the sketch. "So I can hang this anywhere?" she asked with a smile.

"Anywhere you like," replied Nico. "It's also tradition that we get ice cream at the end of the show," he added.

Sonny smiled at her castmates. She was already starting to feel at home. But after all of the excitement of the day, she just wanted to be alone for a few minutes. "I'm going to hang here for a second," she told them.

"All right. We'll see you at the cafeteria, then,"

Grady said. He and Nico headed out of the prop room, leaving Sonny alone.

Sonny smiled to herself but then remembered that she probably hadn't won over Tawni just yet. Oh, well, Sonny thought. It was only an accident and I'm sure she'll forgive me. She should know that I would never do anything to sabotage her. At least I hope she knows that! After all, she's an awesome actress, and I can learn so much from her.

Sonny stood up and walked around the prop house. She still couldn't believe that she was there! She was surrounded by history: the history of *So Random!* and the actors who had starred on the show and made millions of people laugh every week. After all of her years of hard work, she had finally made it! It all seemed too good to be true.

And now, she, Sonny Munroe from Wisconsin, was part of *So Random*'s history, too! She still felt the way she did when she first arrived on the set—like she was dreaming. But she wasn't. All this was real.

Sonny searched for the perfect place to put her bee antennae. And then she found it—right on top of a giant alien figure.

Sonny carefully placed her antennae on the alien's head. Then she used her cell-phone camera to take a picture of herself with the alien. This was a moment she always wanted to remember. It had been one of the most exciting days of her life. And Sonny was sure that there were going to be tons of more exciting days to come!

"I'm on the show!" Sonny said to herself gleefully. "I made *So Random!* I'm on the show! I'm in Hollywood—" Sonny stopped in mid-sentence as Zora suddenly popped out of the coffin in the prop house. "Oh, my gosh!" Sonny cried, startled. Then she burst out laughing.

"Sweet!" Zora cheered. "I'm no longer the weird one!"

Sonny laughed again as Zora retreated back into the coffin. She took one more look around the prop house. Then she ran out to join her new friends.

And there was nothing *random* about that!

PART TWO

CHAPTER 1

The set was finished. The costumes were ready. The audience was seated. The director, producer, cameramen, gaffers, grips, sound techs, prop masters, and all the other important people who make TV shows happen were in their positions behind the scenes. It was time for another taping of the hit sketch comedy show *So Random!*

Tonight, though, there was someone fairly new behind the scenes: a talented girl from Wisconsin, who had followed her dreams all the way to

Hollywood—*So Random!*'s newest cast member, Sonny Munroe. Surrounded by the energetic cast and crew, Sonny's brown eyes twinkled. She'd only been on the show for a few weeks, but Sonny could already tell that the excitement would never wear off.

As the curtain rose and the lights came on, the audience began to applaud.

Sonny took a deep breath. It was time to get the show started! She stepped onto the stage, which was set up like a fast-food restaurant.

"Welcome to Fasty's. What can I get for you?" Grady Mitchell, another member of the cast, asked. He was dressed in a red and black "Fasty's" uniform.

"Hi, I think I'll have a cheeseburger," Sonny told him as she looked over the menu.

Grady leaned into his speaker. "Cheeseburger!" he announced, placing Sonny's order. Suddenly, a cheeseburger came flying at Sonny.

PART I

"Show business is not going to change me,"
Sonny told her mom.

"I'm new," Sonny said, introducing herself to Zora.

"Sorry, I'm a hugger!" Sonny explained to Tawni.

"Stay on your side, don't touch my stuff, and keep *out* of my spotlight," Tawni demanded.

Sonny demonstrated her idea for a new
So Random! sketch. Zora really loved it!

"I got you a little something to say, 'I'm sorry.'
It's a peace offering," Sonny told Tawni.

Sonny had accidentally shredded
Tawni's favorite stuffed cat.

"The first time you star in a sketch, you get to hang
up a prop in the prop house," Grady explained.

PART 2

Sonny couldn't believe that she was talking to
Chad Dylan Cooper, the star of *Mackenzie Falls*!

Everyone was shocked to see the *Mackenzie Falls*
golf cart in their parking spot!

No one except Sonny was excited
for her "peace picnic."

The peace picnic had turned into a disaster!

"I'm going over to the set of *Mackenzie Falls*, and I am *not* coming back without our parking space, our lunch table, and our dignity," Sonny said.

Sonny challenged the cast of *Mackenzie Falls* to a game of musical chairs.

Sonny had won the game!

The cast of *So Random!* gathered to watch Chad give a shout-out to their show on *Mackenzie Falls*!

"Hey! What's the big idea?!" Sonny asked, taken aback.

"Well, most places only offer '*kind* of fast' food," Grady explained. "But here at Fasty's, we specialize in 'really, really, *really* fast' food."

"Yeah, I can see that," Sonny said, peeling a slice of pickle off her shirt.

Grady smiled pleasantly. "Anything else for you?" he asked.

"No, thanks. I don't feel like being hit with chicken bits," Sonny joked.

"Chicken bits!" Grady announced, and before Sonny could duck, she was pelted with chicken nuggets. Frustrated, she turned and left the restaurant.

Then, Tawni Hart, another star of the show, flounced up to the counter. She was dressed in a cheerleading uniform.

"Welcome to Fasty's. May I take your order?" Grady asked.

"Can I just get a salad with dressing on the side?" Tawni asked. As Grady placed the order by speaking into the microphone, lettuce came flying at Tawni—as did the dressing she had ordered. Tawni looked down at her outfit in disgust.

"Good thing I didn't order a soda," she said, rolling her eyes.

"Soda!" Grady called out, and a bucketful of soda was dumped on Tawni's head.

"This is really, really, *really* not cool. If you think I'm paying for this, you're nuts," Tawni told Grady angrily.

"Nuts!" Grady announced as he threw a handful of cashews at Tawni.

"I'm not paying for those nuts either!" Tawni shouted, and stormed out of the restaurant.

Then, Sonny returned. This time, she had come prepared. She was armed with the lid of a garbage can, and she held it in front of her like a shield.

"Hi," she said to Grady. "I was here two seconds ago. You pelted me with chicken bits," she reminded him.

"Chicken bits!" Grady announced, and Sonny shielded herself just in time. Chicken nuggets flew at the garbage-can lid and ricocheted off, bouncing everywhere.

When the coast was clear, Sonny lowered the lid. "I would like to speak to the manager," she told Grady.

"Manager!" Grady called into his microphone.

Just then, their castmate Nico Harris came out of the kitchen. "I'm Mitchell, the manager," he said, smiling at Sonny. "What seems to be the problem?"

"Did you ever stop to think that maybe your restaurant is just a *little* too fast?" Sonny snapped.

"I'm really sorry," Nico said, shaking his head. "Let me make it up to you."

"Thank you," Sonny said gratefully.

"With a year's worth of Fasty's fast fries!" Nico said cheerfully.

"Fast fries!" Grady announced.

"No!" Sonny cried, but it was too late. French fries came flying at her, and not even her garbage-can lid could protect her. When the barrage finally stopped, Sonny lowered the lid. "No ketchup?" she joked.

"Ketchup!" Grady shouted into the micro-phone, and ketchup squirted all over Sonny. She was speechless—and covered in ketchup. She turned and ran out of the restaurant.

"Come again!" Grady called after her.

As the *So Random!* theme music started to play and the curtain fell, the audience clapped and cheered wildly. Behind the curtain, Sonny, Grady, and Nico gave each other high fives. Another successful sketch for the show! Sonny beamed. This was the best job ever!

* * *

After the taping was over, Sonny was already preparing for her next role. She stared at herself in the mirror. Waitress uniform—heavy on the padding? Check. Hair in an updo—heavy on the hairspray? Check. Hand on her hip—heavy on the attitude? Check.

Sonny's transformation into a new character, Madge, the "overworked diner waitress," was complete.

Now all she needed to do was perfect the accent. "All right, now I'm only gonna say this once," Sonny said, practicing in a southern accent. "I got split pea, beef barley, and creamed *tomatah*. Comes with a cracker and a salad. No substitutions!"

Just then, Tawni, still wearing her cheerleader costume, pranced into the room.

"Does this fat suit make me look fat?" Sonny asked, still in character as Madge.

Sonny's *So Random!* castmate raised one perfectly arched eyebrow. "You're in a fat suit?" she said innocently.

Sonny wasn't surprised by Tawni's comment. Since Sonny's first day on the set, Tawni had made it perfectly clear that there was only room for one star on *So Random!*—and that was Tawni Hart.

Sonny tried her best to ignore Tawni. It would take a lot more than Tawni's snide remarks to get rid of her. After all, Sonny hadn't come this far to give up her dream so soon.

"Ha-ha," Sonny replied good-naturedly. "I was going to tell you how great you did in that fast-food sketch, but now I don't think I'm going to."

"You just did," Tawni said with a satisfied smile as she ducked behind a screen to change.

"Darn my niceness," Sonny said to herself.

"Don't blame yourself," Tawni responded.

"It's hard not to compliment me." She reappeared from behind the screen, wearing a bright pink bathrobe with matching slippers and a pink towel around her head.

"I'm sorry," Sonny said in Madge's southern accent. "I couldn't hear you over that robe." She laughed. "I really like playing this character," she said, speaking in her own voice.

"You're playing a character?" Tawni asked innocently again.

"Once again, *ha-ha*," Sonny said. "Now, if anyone needs me before rehearsal, I'll be in the cafeteria getting some frozen yogurt."

"Oh, wait!" Tawni cried out suddenly. "I need you!"

Sonny's eyes widened. Maybe, at last, she'd finally gotten through to Tawni. Maybe Tawni needed her help developing a character or planning a new sketch! Maybe this was about to be the start of the friendly collaboration or best-friendship with Tawni that Sonny had hoped for.

"Really?" Sonny asked eagerly. She knew Tawni would come around!

"Yes. To get me yogurt. Something nondairy and pink," Tawni ordered.

Sonny frowned. "You know I'm not *actually* a waitress, right?" she asked.

Tawni shrugged. "We'll see." She poked her head into the hallway. "Hey, everybody, new girl's making a fro-yo run!"

Zora Lancaster, the youngest star of *So Random!*, popped her head out of an air vent in the ceiling. It was her favorite eavesdropping spot. "I'll take strawberry!" she called.

Suddenly Nico and Grady, still wearing their costumes from the sketch, appeared.

"Cookies and cream!" Grady announced.

"Peanut butter," Nico requested. "And if they don't have peanut butter, grab me a burrito!"

"Oh, I'm in for a burrito, too," added Grady. He and Nico were both known for having hearty appetites.

Zora popped her head through another air vent. "I need twelve double-A batteries," she told Sonny.

"See?" Tawni commented. "You *are* a waitress," she said haughtily, tossing her hair over her shoulder.

Sonny grinned. Some people might be annoyed by suddenly having to fetch orders for four teen stars. But Sonny was trying to look on the bright side. She saw it as a great opportunity to practice her Madge character. And since she was the newest member of the *So Random!* team, she needed all the practice she could get!

"O-*kay*," Sonny said in Madge's southern voice. She thought for a moment. "Let me see if I've got this. That's one no-moo any pink, one straw, one creamy-cook, one p-b-slash-'rito, one

69

'rito walkin', and twelve double-A's." She smiled proudly. She was really getting the hang of this!

"And instead of a yogurt I actually would like—" Tawni began.

Sonny held up her hand. "No substitutions!" she barked in Madge's voice.

CHAPTER
2

A few minutes later, Sonny was standing in front of the frozen-yogurt machine in the studio cafeteria. Her tray was loaded with burritos and cups of frozen yogurt. As she filled her fifth frozen-yogurt cup, Sonny started wondering how Madge would stand. Would she slouch over? Would she stand proudly and rest her tray against her hip?

But before she could practice any poses for her new character, Sonny was interrupted by a tall, handsome guy with thick blond hair and dazzling blue eyes.

"Excuse me, miss," he said. "When you're done with that order, I'm going to need an extra-large chocolate."

Startled, Sonny turned around. "Oh, I don't work here," she began. But as she looked at the cute guy standing next to her, Sonny realized that he looked familiar. "Oh, my gosh! I know you," she said as it dawned on her. "You're . . . you're . . ." She was so starstruck, she couldn't even speak.

"Him." The boy finished her sentence, pointing at a massive poster for the show *Mackenzie Falls*. "Chad Dylan Cooper." He flashed her a wide smile.

Sonny's mouth dropped open. "You're Mackenzie on *Mackenzie Falls*!" she exclaimed.

"And apparently you're Madge," Chad replied as he read the name tag on Sonny's costume.

"Yes," Sonny replied in a daze. She couldn't believe she was face-to-face with *the* Chad Dylan Cooper, the most handsome and popular teen actor on TV! His looks were legendary, and not a week passed by that he wasn't on the cover of some celebrity magazine.

Then Sonny realized what she had just said. "No! No!" she continued. She tried to keep her composure. "Madge is my waitress character. And all of *this* belongs to Madge, too," she added, patting the padding in her uniform. "I'm Sonny."

"Sonny," Chad said with a grin. "That's a nice name." He pulled a photograph of himself out of his back pocket and started to write on it.

Sonny couldn't stop staring at Chad. "Thank you!" she exclaimed. "You know, when I was young, I didn't really like it, but now I think it kind of suits me," Sonny began to ramble. There was no denying it: she was officially starstruck! "I mean I have this one friend, and her name is—"

"Here you go," Chad interrupted as he handed Sonny the photo. He was used to having this effect on girls.

"'Sonny, thanks for the yogurt, Chad Dylan Cooper,'" Sonny read the inscription aloud. Then she stopped. "Hey, I didn't give you any—"

But by the time she looked up, Chad Dylan Cooper was halfway across the cafeteria—carrying away the entire tray of frozen yogurt that Sonny had picked up for her castmates!

"Hey!" she yelled. "Chad Dylan Cooper just stole my yogurt!"

Then a huge smile spread across her face. "Oh, my gosh! Chad Dylan Cooper just stole my yogurt!" she squealed excitedly.

A few minutes later, Sonny returned to the *So Random!* prop house. It was the storage room for all the props that had been used during the show's comedy sketches. It was filled with reminders of *So Random!*'s amazing history, which made the room an awesome hangout for the cast when they weren't rehearsing or working on new comedy routines.

"Sorry I'm late," Sonny said as she handed everyone what they had requested. She was still grinning from her unexpected meeting with Chad Dylan Cooper. "Here you go."

"My yogurt's melted," Grady said with a frown.

"My burrito's cold," Nico said, wrinkling his nose.

"These are *triple*-A!" groaned Zora as Sonny handed her a package of batteries that were the wrong size.

"And I *didn't* order sprinkles," Tawni complained as she took a bite of her frozen yogurt.

"Oh, yeah, those aren't sprinkles," Sonny said apologetically. "I kind of dropped it in the parking lot."

Tawni grimaced as she crunched down on pieces of gravel and dirt.

"My bad!" Sonny continued. "But you'll totally forgive me when you find out who I just met!" She proudly pulled out the photo that Chad had given her moments before. "Chad Dylan Cooper!"

Zora, Tawni, Nico, and Grady gasped in shock.

"I *know*!" Sonny exclaimed excitedly. "Chad Dylan Cooper!"

Once again, the rest of the cast gasped. But this time, Grady grabbed the picture out of Sonny's hands.

"Sonny!" he cried. "This three-name doofus is the enemy. We do *not* associate with him or anybody on *Mackenzie Falls*!"

"And now we have melted yogurt and cold burritos because of . . . I can't even say his name," Nico added bitterly.

Sonny shook her head. "No," she replied. "We have melted yogurt because I had to walk so far from where I parked the golf cart."

"You took the golf cart?!" Grady asked, a look of horror on his face.

"Say it ain't so!" Zora cried.

"Yeah, it was right out front, so I figured I'd take it for a spin," Sonny said, not seeing what the problem was.

"Say it ain't so!" Zora said again in disbelief.

"What's the big deal?" Sonny asked. "Isn't it there for taking and spinning?"

"Say it ain't so!" Zora repeated a third time, now panicked.

"Easy Z, easy," cautioned Nico as he put his hand on her arm.

Tawni's eyes narrowed as she stared at Sonny. "When you came back, whose cart was in our space?" she asked in an icy tone.

"Well . . . it was . . . uh . . ." stammered Sonny.

"Whose cart?" yelled the rest of the cast together.

With Tawni, Zora, Grady, and Nico following right behind her, Sonny ran into the hallway to look out the window.

Outside, a terrible scene met their eyes. The parking spot—the coveted, right-next-to-the-door parking spot—was occupied by another golf cart. And the golf cart was surrounded by a dozen teenage actors, laughing and grinning.

It was the cast of *Mackenzie Falls*, and in the middle was Chad Dylan Cooper himself. They waved, gloating, at Sonny and her friends.

The *So Random!* cast walked dejectedly back to the prop house, but Sonny still didn't understand why everyone was so upset. "What's the big deal?" she asked. "They'll move their cart later, and we'll get our space back."

"You are *so* naïve," Tawni hissed. "They'll

never move their cart. *Our* cart was parked there for two years."

Two years?! Sonny thought. What was the point of having a golf cart if you were going to leave it sitting in a parking lot for two years? "It's just a parking space," she replied, confused.

"This isn't about a parking space," Grady tried to explain. "This is about something bigger. This is about *Mackenzie Falls* thinking they're so much better than us just because they're *'real'* actors on a drama show and we're just 'funny.'"

"And they're all high-and-mighty with their perfect skin and fancy clothes and windswept hair," added Nico.

"I mean, I have all those things, and they *still* look down on me," Tawni said.

"Oh, come on, guys—is it really that bad?" asked Sonny.

"Tell her, Nico," Zora said solemnly. "Tell her what she needs to hear."

"It was two years ago," Nico said seriously. "*Mackenzie Falls* beat us out for the prestigious Tween Choice award. And if that wasn't crushing enough, afterward there was . . . the interview."

Nico closed his eyes. He could remember the interview as clearly as if it had happened yesterday: smug Chad Dylan Cooper celebrating the award that *should* have gone to *So Random!* And worst of all, Chad hadn't bothered to hide his true feelings for their show when he spoke about the award.

"You know, a lot of people would say that it's '*so random*' that we won this award," Chad had gloated to a room full of cameras. "But it's not 'so random' at all. It's never 'so random' because *Mackenzie Falls* rules! Thank you, tweens!"

"But we showed them," Grady continued, picking up where Nico had trailed off. "We took their parking spot—"

"*And* stole their Tween Choice award,"

80

finished Tawni, "which we now use as a toilet-paper holder!" Tawni, Zora, Grady, and Nico all laughed.

But Sonny didn't think the story was that funny. In fact, she thought it was kind of mean-spirited.

"Look, you guys, I know I'm the new girl—" Sonny started to say.

"Bored already," Tawni interrupted her, faking a yawn.

"And I can see how upset you all are," continued Sonny. "But aren't you tired of the fighting? Isn't it time to bury the hatchet?"

"A hatchet!" Zora exclaimed. "That's what we need!"

"No, Zora," Sonny said, shaking her head. "It's time to end the feud."

"That's what the hatchet's for!" Zora replied. And with that, she raced off to look for one.

Sonny decided to try another approach.

"Look, back in Wisconsin, my school had a rivalry with a snooty prep school. They thought they were better than us. And after a while, we started to believe it. Finally, I said, 'Enough!' And you know what I did about it?"

Sonny looked at her castmates expectantly, but they stared blankly back at her.

"I'll tell you what I did," Sonny went on. "I organized a 'peace picnic.' There were games and food, and by the end of the day, enemies became friends, and we *all* felt better about ourselves."

"If I ran myself over with a golf cart, it would *still* be less painful than that story," Tawni replied.

Suddenly, from another part of the prop house, Zora called out, "I found a hatchet!"

"Guys, come on!" pleaded Sonny. "Let the picnic work its magic. Trust me, there's no problem my egg salad can't solve!"

"Tell that to Chad Dylan Cooper," Nico scoffed.

And with that, the rest of the *So Random!* cast exited the prop house, leaving Sonny to figure out how to end the rivalry with *Mackenzie Falls* once and for all.

CHAPTER
3

Later that afternoon, Sonny was standing back to admire some of her work. The *So Random!* table in the studio cafeteria was adorned with tons of peace-inspired decorations, such as peace signs and a large white stuffed dove that Sonny had found in the prop house.

In addition to the decorations, the table was loaded with delicious picnic food: a platter piled high with sandwiches, a tray of deviled eggs, a mountain of cupcakes, and large bowls of fruit salad, potato salad, pasta salad, and Sonny's specialty—egg salad.

Sonny couldn't help but smile. She was pretty proud of herself. "I don't mean to brag, but this has the makings of being the best peace picnic in the history of peace picnics!" she exclaimed. "Now, Grady, if you don't mind, please set down the peace offering on the 'podium of peace.'"

Grady stepped forward, carrying the Tween Choice award that the cast of *So Random!* had stolen from the *Mackenzie Falls* stars two long years before. It still had a roll of toilet paper stuck on its arm.

"Now, Grady, if you don't mind, please remove the toilet paper from the peace offering," Sonny requested politely.

With a sigh, Grady pulled the toilet paper off the statue.

"Perfect!" Sonny cried happily. "Now, our

guests will be here any minute, so let's take a seat. Let the peace begin!"

Sonny sat down at the table. The rest of the cast reluctantly followed her example.

And that's when disaster struck.

Everything seemed to happen in slow motion.

The table collapsing.

The food flying everywhere.

The egg salad spilling all over Sonny's head.

They hadn't quite figured it out yet, but the cast of *So Random!* knew that something was very, very wrong. Then they tried to stand up—only to discover that they were stuck to their seats with superglue!

"I'm stuck!" Grady cried in shock.

"Dude, we've been glued to our chairs!" yelled Nico.

"*Mackenzie Falls* did this," Zora said, seething.

Sonny stood up, the chair still glued to her.

Her dreams of a peace picnic with the cast of *Mackenzie Falls* had been shattered. "At least we still have their statue," she pointed out.

Suddenly, Chad Dylan Cooper ran through the cafeteria. He grabbed the Tween Choice award from the podium of peace. "Woo-hoo! Peace out!" he called with a laugh.

Sonny tried to remain calm as she wiped egg salad out of her eyes. "Well, at least we still have our dignity," she said.

Grady tried to stand up again.

Rrrrrrrip!

Unfortunately, he had attempted to stand too quickly, ripping his jeans in the process. The chair fell to the ground, taking the seat of his pants with it!

Just then, a *Mackenzie Falls* cast member popped into the room with a digital camera and began snapping away.

Sonny was desperate to find something

87

positive about this awful situation. "At least we still have—"

"Nothing!" screamed Zora. "We have *nothing*!"

The next day, Sonny showed up for rehearsal bright and early. She was full of hope that her fellow cast members would have forgiven her for the peace picnic fiasco—but she was carrying a basket of homemade muffins, just in case.

"Morning, everybody!" she called out in an overly cheerful voice. "I hope you're not still mad at me!"

THWACK!

Sonny reeled as a piece of ham hit her directly on the side of the face.

"It works!" Zora cheered. "My cold-cut catapult works!"

"Okay, ham on my face," Sonny said as she peeled the slice of meat off her cheek. "I suppose

I deserved that." Then her voice became cheery again. "But you guys know what *you* deserve? Home-baked cranberry muffins, fresh from—" Sonny suddenly stopped midsentence. She glanced at the computer screen her castmates were staring at. "Is that Grady's butt?" she asked in shock.

"It is indeed," Nico said coldly. "Thanks to your stupid peace picnic, it's all over the Internet. Two million hits."

"Well, you know what they say," Sonny joked, "there's no such thing as bad butt-blicity! Am I right?"

THWACK!

A slice of cheese landed on Sonny's face.

"I see the cold-cut catapult also works with cheese," Sonny remarked as she peeled the slice off her cheek.

"Guys, come on," Tawni spoke up. "Hasn't she suffered enough?"

Everyone looked over at Tawni in surprise. It wasn't like her to be sympathetic to anyone! With a sly grin, Tawni continued, "Yeah, I didn't think so, either. Check this out!"

A few clicks of the mouse later, and the cast gathered around the computer screen. There in slow motion was a running stream of hidden-camera video footage of Sonny being splattered with a whole bowl of egg salad.

"Is that *me*?" Sonny asked, horrified.

"Oh, yes," Tawni replied smugly.

"Over and over and over again," Sonny said as the video began to repeat. She felt her face grow hot—partly from embarrassment and partly from anger.

"You know what they say," said Grady. "There's no such thing as bad egg salad–blicity! Am I right?"

"Okay, that's *it*!" Sonny announced angrily. "*Now* it's personal! I'm going over to *Mackenzie*

Falls, and I promise I'm not coming back—"

"Yay!" cheered Tawni, interrupting her. She clapped her hands.

But Sonny hadn't finished. "Without our parking space, our lunch table, *and* our dignity!"

As Sonny turned to leave, Zora loaded up the catapult again.

This time, though, Sonny was ready. She grabbed the flying piece of ham out of the air before it could hit her in the face.

Nothing could stop her now!

CHAPTER
4

Across the studio on the *Mackenzie Falls* set, Chad Dylan Cooper was in the zone. He knew that girls swooned over the romantic scenes he performed as Mackenzie, and he wanted this one to be just right.

Chad was sitting next to a pretty young actress who played Mackenzie's girlfriend, Portlyn. Or, rather, Mackenzie's soon-to-be *ex*-girlfriend. Her eyes filled with tears as Chad gazed into them.

"Look, Portlyn," he said, his voice full of emotion. "Summer's almost over. And once fall comes back to the Falls, I need to be free." He ran his hands through his hair and gave her a serious look.

Portlyn tried to speak, but Chad pressed his finger to her lips. "Shhh," he whispered. "The time for talking is over." He looked at her meaningfully.

Just then, Sonny burst onto the set. She was furious at Chad, and ready to confront him. She didn't care that he was in the middle of a scene. "What's the *matter* with you?" she shouted at the top of her lungs.

Chad was so deeply in character that he didn't even notice Sonny at first. Still staring at Portlyn, he replied, "What's the matter with *me*? What's the matter with—wait, those words didn't come out of your mouth," Chad said in confusion.

"Cut!" the director suddenly yelled. Bright lights flooded the set, and the cameras stopped rolling.

Chad stood up and turned to face Sonny. "We're *sort of* in the middle of a shoot here," he said haughtily. If there was one thing Chad didn't like, it was to be interrupted during a scene.

"And now you're *sort of* taking a break," Sonny retorted.

The actress playing Portlyn stood up and scurried off the set. She didn't want to get in the middle of this argument!

"Stay sad, sweetie!" Chad called after her. Then he turned back to Sonny and frowned. "What's your problem?"

Sonny's face was flushed with anger. "My problem is that everything my friends—*and* Tawni—told me about you was true," she barked. "You *Mackenzie Falls* guys are jerks. And you're the head jerk, the mayor of Jerkville, the ambassador of Jerkoslovakia, the—"

Chad's eyes twinkled mischievously. "You saw the egg-salad video," he said, smiling with satisfaction. "I also direct."

"We were trying to make peace!" Sonny exclaimed.

"Please," Chad said dismissively. "You were trying to trap us." He looked at her suspiciously and frowned.

"Trap you?" Sonny repeated. "You've *obviously* been watching your own show too much. You know, not everything is cutthroat and gossipy. Sometimes, people do things because they're trying to be nice." She couldn't believe that Chad didn't trust her. I guess that's Hollywood for you, she thought.

As Sonny continued to yell at Chad for what he had done, a lighting assistant started fiddling with the lights. Suddenly, the set was bathed in beautiful blue moonlight. A backdrop of a grassy hill and a full moon was placed behind the two of them. It might have seemed romantic—if Sonny and Chad weren't glaring at each other.

"Do they, Sonny? Do they *really*?" Chad asked dramatically. "Look, it was sweet of you to put that picnic together. It was *way* sweet," Chad said, as the fake moon rose high in the sky. "But the bad blood between our two shows has run too deep for too long to be healed by a bowl of egg salad and even the best of intentions," Chad continued. He reached for Sonny's hand. "Just because you wish for something doesn't make it so."

Just then, stars in the backdrop began to twinkle. The moon began to glow. Sonny started to get carried away by the romantic scenery and lighting—and by the fact that the very handsome Chad Dylan Cooper was holding her hand and staring at her with his piercing blue eyes. She gulped. What was she saying again?

"I must go," he said softly. "So run, run back to your show. Put your sweet little dreams of peace to bed."

Chad gave Sonny one more long, meaningful look. And then, he turned on his heel and slowly walked away.

Beneath the fake stars, in the fake light of the fake moon, with the fake breeze ruffling her hair, Sonny suddenly felt confused. "What just happened?" she asked.

But Chad was already gone. And Sonny was more conflicted than ever.

Sonny went back to her dressing room to try and figure out what had just happened with Chad. She hoped she'd have a few minutes to herself so she could gather her thoughts.

But that was impossible when the entire cast of *So Random!* was looking for her. As Sonny heard voices in the hallway, she let out a sigh. I guess I better deal with them now, she thought.

"There she is!" Zora announced as she banged open the door.

"Hey, guys!" Sonny said brightly. Maybe if she pretended nothing had happened, her castmates wouldn't ask her any questions and would forget that she told them she was going to talk to Chad. "Where have you been?"

"Where have *we* been?" Grady asked. "Where have *you* been?"

Sonny tried to stall for time. "I asked you first!" she said defensively.

Nico pushed his way to the front of the group. "What happened with Chad?" he demanded, giving her a serious look.

"Well . . ." Sonny said slowly. She looked around frantically. She had to come up with something, and quick! Then she spotted a hair dryer on the dressing table. That gave her a great idea. Casually, Sonny picked it up.

"I went over there," she began to tell the group. "And—"

Just then, Sonny turned on the hair dryer.

VRRRRRRRRRRRRRRRR!

With the hair dryer on full blast, Sonny could tell her friends the whole story—but they wouldn't hear a word! *Am I good or am I good?* she thought.

After a few moments, she turned the hair dryer off again. "And that's why everything's okay," she finished with a smile. She hoped that this would be the end of the conversation.

"Did you get back our—" Grady started to ask.

VRRRRRRRRRRRRRRRR! Sonny turned the hair dryer back on to drown out the rest of his question.

Zora, however, knew exactly what Sonny was trying to do. She yanked the plug out of the wall, and the device went silent. "Start talking," she ordered.

"Well, it's an interesting story," Sonny said with a nervous laugh.

"Did it go something like this?" Tawni asked, feigning interest. "Blah, blah, blah, peace picnic. Blah, blah, blah, I got nothing," she said, clearly making fun of Sonny.

"First of all, that sounds nothing like me," Sonny said indignantly. "And secondly, I *did* get something."

Tawni raised an eyebrow. "Really? What?" she asked.

"I got . . . an agreement," Sonny replied, still unsure of herself.

"An agreement for what?" Nico asked slowly.

"An agreement that says . . . if we . . . beat them at something . . . we . . . get all our stuff back," Sonny stammered, hoping no one could tell she was making all of this up as she went along.

100

"Beat them at what?" Grady asked, wrinkling his nose.

"Something . . . we're good at," Sonny said slowly.

"Like what?" Grady pressed. "Musical chairs?"

Sonny's eyes lit up. "Are we good at that?" she asked eagerly.

Sonny's castmates looked at her suspiciously. She looked back at them with a hopeful smile. Maybe this could work after all! she thought.

CHAPTER
5

Sonny clenched her fists and gritted her teeth as she approached the *Mackenzie Falls* set. She had to convince Chad to agree to the musical-chairs challenge—there was no way she could go back to the *So Random!* cast and admit that she'd made up the whole story. This time, Sonny was ready to confront him on his own turf. She wouldn't let any lighting tricks, special effects, or television magic interfere with her latest plan. Not even Chad's gorgeous blue eyes would stand in her way!

Sonny found him on set, sitting back in a comfortable chair as a makeup artist carefully applied powder to his face. Chad raised an eyebrow as Sonny walked into the room. He listened quietly while Sonny explained the musical-chairs challenge.

When she finished talking, Chad remained silent. At last, he replied, "Musical chairs? You're challenging us to *musical chairs*?"

"You heard me," Sonny said calmly.

"That's a game for children between the ages of four and seven," Chad scoffed.

"Which makes it suitable for you," Sonny shot back.

Chad reached forward to grab a bottle of water. "Look, I don't know how much free time you have over there in 'Chuckle City,' but over here on *Mackenzie Falls*, we have some serious acting to do," he said.

"Oh, my gosh!" Sonny exclaimed. "You *are* a drama snob. You *do* think you're better than us!"

"Not better," Chad corrected her. "Just different . . . in a better way: we *act*."

A smile spread across Sonny's face. "I see what's going on here," she replied. "You're afraid we might be better than you at something."

Chad stood up. "I'm not afraid of anything," he replied arrogantly.

"Except musical chairs," Sonny teased.

"*Especially* not musical chairs," Chad said firmly.

"Fine, then here are the terms," Sonny said. "We win, we get our parking spot back, we get *your* table in the cafeteria, and you have to buy us a new toilet-paper holder."

"We're not doing that," Chad said, shaking his head.

"Then I guess you *are* afraid," Sonny said,

shrugging. She decided to turn on the pressure with her best chicken impression. *"Bawk! Bawk! Bawk!"* she clucked.

"Stop it," Chad said. "You're acting like a fool."

"Actually, I'm acting like a chicken. I'm not afraid to act like a fool," Sonny corrected him. *"Bawk, bawk, bawk, bawk, bawk—"*

"Cut it out!" Chad ordered. "There are people starting to stare!"

But Sonny just ignored him. She continued bawking as she strutted around flapping her arms like chicken wings.

"Stop!" Chad cried. "Fine, we'll do it, okay? And when *we* win, you have to go on your show and say that *Mackenzie Falls* is better than *So Random!*"

"Fine, but when *we* win, you have to say something nice about *So Random!*," Sonny countered.

"No, no, no!" Chad said. "We're not doing that. You already told me your terms. You don't get to keep adding stuff."

"Bawk! Bawk! Bawk!" Sonny squawked loudly.

"Fine! Okay! Deal!" Chad yelled. "Musical chairs."

"See you at noon," said Sonny, smiling with satisfaction. She turned to go. This has to work, she thought. It just *has* to.

CHAPTER 6

At lunchtime, Sonny, Nico, Grady, and Zora went to the cafeteria to get ready for the competition. Each one of them was wearing a SAY NO TO THE *FALLS* shirt with a crossed-out picture of Chad's face on it. The group cleared some tables out of the way and arranged nine chairs in a circle. When the *Mackenzie Falls* cast showed up, the members of *So Random!* would be ready for them!

"I can't believe we're playing musical chairs,"

Grady muttered as he rolled his eyes.

"Grady, you said we were good at this," Sonny reminded him.

"I said this is what we were *best* at, I didn't say we were *good* at it," he replied.

"Come on, you guys!" Sonny exclaimed, trying to rally them. "We can do this. Don't let them psych us out! We just need to practice. Okay, everybody, on your feet!"

Nico, Grady, and Zora reluctantly dragged themselves up from their chairs.

Sonny started marching in place. "Okay, we're walking, we're walking, we're walking—*sit*!" She suddenly sat down, demonstrating how they would practice. "Now, everybody with me!"

The cast followed her movements.

"Walking, walking, walking—*sit*! Walking, walking, walking—*sit*!" Everyone chanted in unison.

Suddenly, Sonny had a strange feeling that

she was being watched. She looked up—and saw Chad and the rest of the *Mackenzie Falls* cast standing in the doorway, smirking at her and her castmates.

Chad faked a yawn. "Let's get this over with," he said. "I have to get my teeth bleached in twenty minutes. Did you know there are eighty shades of white?"

Just then, Tawni sauntered into the room. She was wearing the same SAY NO TO THE *FALLS* shirt as the rest of the cast—except hers was decorated with beads, sequins, and a fancy feathered collar. "Did we win? Did we lose? Is it over? Can I leave?" she asked hopefully.

"No, we need you. We're a team," Sonny answered her. "Let's do this!"

A stagehand from *Mackenzie Falls* hoisted a giant boom box onto a table. Slowly, dramatically, he pressed PLAY. The cafeteria was flooded with music.

And the game was on!

The casts of *So Random!* and *Mackenzie Falls* raced around the chairs, each person hoping to have a seat when the music stopped.

Suddenly, without warning, the stagehand cut the music.

Everyone scrambled frantically for the chairs—everyone, that is, except Tawni. She didn't even try to sit in a chair. Instead, she stood apart from the group, examining her nails. "Oh, no, I lost," she said in a bored voice. "Toodles!" She turned and walked out of the room.

The music started up again. Everyone began to circle the chairs once more. Then the music stopped.

As everyone dove for a chair, Nico stood aside. "After you," he said politely, offering his seat to the actress who played Portlyn.

As the girl sat down, she flashed Nico a dazzling smile. Then Nico suddenly realized what he had done. "Aw, man!" he exclaimed.

Now there were only three *So Random!* cast members left in the game. And the *Mackenzie Falls* team hadn't lost a player!

The music started up again, and Grady was determined to stay in the game. He started chanting to himself, "Walking, walking, walking, walking . . ." so that he would stay focused.

But when the music stopped, Grady was still repeating his mantra—and that's exactly what he kept doing!

"Oh, man! I forgot to sit," he groaned.

Things were not looking good for the *So Random!* team. They only had two players left—Sonny and Zora!

Then their luck seemed to turn around. The music played for a while, and when it stopped, a *Mackenzie Falls* player was left without a chair. Then another one! The teams were finally starting to even out, with three players from

111

Mackenzie Falls and two from *So Random!* left.

Everyone was focused now. When the music stopped again, Zora and Portlyn dove for the same chair.

THWACK! Suddenly, a flying piece of meat landed smack on Portlyn's face!

Sonny looked over and spotted Tawni, who had snuck back into the room. She was manning Zora's cold-cut catapult, and her aim—right at Portlyn's head—was perfect.

"You're *helping*?" Sonny asked Tawni in surprise.

Tawni shrugged, trying to act nonchalant. But deep down, she really did want to beat *Mackenzie Falls*.

The game continued until only Sonny and Chad were left. One chair stood between them.

Whoever got that chair would win it all:

The glory.

The bragging rights.

The parking space.

The music began to play once more. Slowly—*very* slowly—Sonny and Chad began to circle the chair, never taking their eyes off each other.

"Looks like it's just you, me, and one more thing you're not going to get," Chad said to Sonny.

"You're acting pretty confident for somebody who's going to lose," she retorted.

"At least I can act," Chad replied.

"Can you, Chad?" Sonny asked. "Can you *really*?"

From the sidelines, Nico let out a low whistle. "You see that?" he said to his castmates. "She's giving it right back to him."

"We might actually win," Tawni marveled.

"We could have a toilet-paper holder by sundown!" exclaimed Grady.

"Come on, Sonny!" Zora cheered.

"Yes! Yes! Yes!" chanted Grady, Nico, Tawni, and Zora.

113

Suddenly, the music stopped. Sonny rushed for the chair, but she suddenly fell to the ground, shrieking in pain.

"Ow!" she cried out.

"Noooo!" howled Grady, Nico, Tawni, and Zora.

"My ankle!" Sonny moaned. "It really hurts! I think something snapped!"

Chad leaned over Sonny, a look of genuine concern on his face. "Oh, man," he said anxiously. "That looks really serious. We'd better get you to a doctor. Take my hand."

Chad held out his hand to Sonny. She grabbed it—and pulled him to the ground! Then she leaped over him and landed right in the chair!

"Peace out!" Sonny yelled triumphantly.

The *So Random!* cast erupted in cheers and shouts.

"You tricked me!" Chad exclaimed, picking himself up off the floor.

Sonny shook her head. "Nope," she replied. "I was *acting*."

Chad couldn't help smiling. "Not bad," he admitted. "Perhaps there's a spot for you on *Mackenzie Falls*," he said.

Sonny grinned at Chad. "Thanks, but my home is right here in Chuckle City, on a show called *So Random!* So I don't think I'll go anywhere, Chad Dylan Cooper."

She smiled widely. Not bad for a Hollywood newbie, she thought proudly.

The next night, Sonny, Grady, Nico, Zora, and Tawni gathered around the TV in the prop house. Everybody had a big bowl of frozen yogurt—not melted this time, and *not* covered in gravel from the parking lot.

It was time for *Mackenzie Falls*. The cast of *So Random!* had never convened to watch their rivals before.

But tonight promised to be the best episode ever!

No one spoke as the camera zoomed in on Chad's face. Beside him stood Portlyn, her eyes full of tears. Chad placed his hands on her shoulders and gazed deeply into her eyes.

"Look, Portlyn, summer's almost over," he said dramatically. "And once fall comes back to the Falls, I need to be free."

Portlyn tried to speak, but Chad put his finger to her lips.

"Shhh," he whispered. "The time for talking is over. Because . . ."

Chad paused, his face clouded with emotion. He looked devastated as he choked out the rest of the line.

"The time for talking is over because *So Random!* is on," he finally muttered. "It's my favorite show."

The cast of *So Random!* burst into laughter

and high-fived one another. Chad might not have been telling the truth—but with his "true" acting skills, no one in the world would ever know!

Sonny smiled to herself. After all they'd been through, she was starting to think that Chad wasn't such a bad guy—even though he could be a little conceited sometimes. She wondered if she'd run into him again by the frozen-yogurt machine. Hopefully, she wouldn't be wearing her Madge costume this time.

But even if she was, Sonny wouldn't care. She wouldn't trade her spot on *So Random!* for anything!

Hollywood is calling!
Look for the next book in the
Sonny With A Chance series.

making
the Cut

Adapted by N. B. Grace

Based on the series created by Steve Marmel

Based on the episode, "Promises, Prom-misses," Written by Dava Savel

Sonny Munroe had just left the set of *So Random!*, the popular sketch-comedy show that she was currently starring in. She was so busy looking down at her phone that she didn't see where she was going. "I can't believe I missed it," she said to herself with a sigh.

"Whoa, watch it!" a voice suddenly yelled out.

Sonny looked up in surprise to see Chad Dylan Cooper, the supercute star of *Mackenzie Falls*, a romantic teen drama that filmed nearby. Even though she had a little bit of a crush on him, she would never admit it to anyone. And he was way too arrogant for Sonny to ever really take him seriously.

"I'm so sorry," Sonny began to say. Then she noticed that Chad had a huge bruise on his face. "Oh, my gosh!" she exclaimed. "What happened?"

"I just got in a huge fight over at *Mackenzie Falls*," Chad said nonchalantly. "We were shooting a scene. I know, it's hard to believe I could look this good when I look this bad, huh?" he said, pushing his blond hair out of his eyes. "What's up with you?"

"Nothing," Sonny said, a hint of disappointment in her voice. "I missed my prom back home, and I just got some pictures from my best friend, so . . ." she told him, her voice trailing off.

Chad shrugged. "You're not missing much. I've been to a bunch of proms, and they've all ended in disaster," he told Sonny.

"Oh, I'm sorry to hear that," Sonny said sympathetically.

"Yeah, episode ten, my hair caught on fire. Last year's season finale, my date turned out to be my long-lost sister," Chad stated, shaking his head.

Sonny looked at him in confusion. "What?" she asked. "Uh, Chad, those are fake proms."

Chad rolled his eyes. "Fake proms, real proms, they all stink."

"No, they don't!" Sonny exclaimed. "They're romantic! You know, a girl dreams her whole life about going to the prom and having that perfect dance with a very special guy," she said dreamily.

Chad yawned. "Then he gets hit on the head by a faulty disco ball. Episode sixteen," he said.

Sonny couldn't believe what she was hearing.

Even though she was pretty new to the West Coast, having just recently moved from a small town in Wisconsin, she couldn't believe that Chad wasn't the tiniest bit interested in going to a prom. These Hollywood types were proving to be too much!

"You know what, Chad?" she told him. "You wouldn't know a real romance if it punched you in the face. In fact, you wouldn't know a real *punch* in the face if it punched you in the face, because there's nothing real about you!" she shouted.

Chad's eyes narrowed. "Oh, well, here's something real for you. I really don't want to stand here and talk to you!" he retorted.

"Good!" Sonny shot back. "Because I really don't want to stand here and talk to you!" And with that, she stomped away.

Ugh! Sonny thought as she tried to calm down. This day was turning out to be a disaster!